BIONICLE®

Adventures
Sampler

BIONICLE®

*FIND THE POWER,
LIVE THE LEGEND*

The legend comes alive in these exciting BIONICLE® books:

BIONICLE® Chronicles

#1: Tale of the Toa

#2: Beware the Bohrok

#3: Makuta's Revenge

#4: Tales of the Masks

The Official Guide to BIONICLE™

BIONICLE™ Collector's Sticker Book

BIONICLE™: Mask of Light

BIONICLE® Adventures

#1: Mystery of Metru Nui

#2: Trial by Fire

#3: The Darkness Below

#4: Legends of Metru Nui

#5: Voyage of Fear

COMING SOON

#6: Maze of Shadows

BIONICLE®

Adventures
Sampler

by Greg Farshtey

SCHOLASTIC INC.
New York Toronto London Auckland Sydney
Mexico City New Delhi Hong Kong Buenos Aires

Bionicle® Adventures #1: Mystery of Metru Nui, ISBN 0-439-60731-0,
Copyright © 2003 by The LEGO Group.

Bionicle® Adventures #2: Trial by Fire, ISBN 0-439-60732-9,
Copyright © 2003 by The LEGO Group.

Bionicle® Adventures #3: The Darkness Below, ISBN 0-439-60733-7,
Copyright © 2004 by The LEGO Group.

Bionicle® Adventures #4: Legends of Metru Nui, ISBN 0-439-62747-8,
Copyright © 2004 by The LEGO Group.

ISBN 0-439-73460-6

12 11 10 9 8 7 6 5 4 3 2 1   4 5 6 7 8 9/0

Printed in the U.S.A.   40

First compilation printing, September 2004

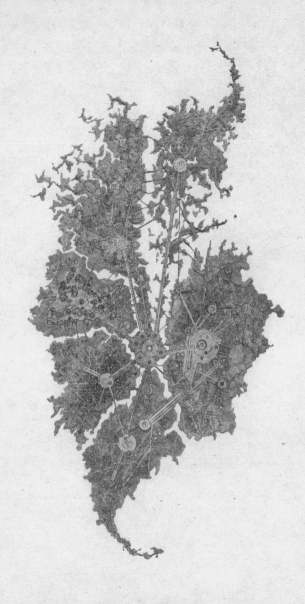

The City of Metru Nui

BIONICLE®

Adventures #1

Mystery of Metru Nui

INTRODUCTION

Turaga Vakama, elder of the Mata Nui village of fire, stood on a high cliff overlooking the beach. Far below, Matoran from all over the island were hard at work constructing boats for the long journey back home.

Vakama shook his head. Home. It had been so long since any of them had seen it, and the Matoran did not even remember living anywhere but Mata Nui. Only the six village elders recalled when and why they first came to the island, and for thousands of years, they had locked that secret away inside themselves.

The Turaga turned at the sound of another's approach. It was Tahu Nuva, Toa of Fire and leader of the heroes of Mata Nui. "How go the labors, Turaga?" he asked.

"Quite well, Toa Tahu. We will soon have enough boats to carry us all back to the island city of Metru Nui. The Po-Matoran are at work widening the tunnels so we can carry the boats to the subterranean sea."

Tahu nodded as his mind flashed back to the events of the past months. After the final confrontation with Makuta, master of shadows, the Toa had discovered a new island far beneath the surface of Mata Nui. It sat in the center of a silver sea of protodermis, and they could see few details of it from the shore. But Vakama insisted that this place was Metru Nui, the original home of the Matoran, to which they must return.

Even more startling, the Turaga revealed that Metru Nui had once been home to six other Toa, heroes who existed long before Tahu and the others ever appeared. But Vakama had said nothing about the fate of those early "Toa Metru," or whether they might still be waiting on Metru Nui.

"I have been in council with the other Toa,"

said Tahu. "I have come to ask you to tell us all about this new land, Metru Nui. If we are going to journey there and protect the Matoran from any threats that might lurk in that place, we must know everything."

Vakama turned and walked away from the cliff. "Indeed you must. But I will warn you, Tahu: The tales of Metru Nui are tales of sacrifice, betrayal, great danger, and yes, heroes as well. Their telling may change much of what you think you know about myself, the other Turaga, and the Matoran you have served all this time."

"I — we — are prepared for that, Turaga," replied Tahu. "The Toa have gathered at the Great Temple of Kini-Nui. They wait only for you."

"Then let them wait no longer, Tahu."

The seven Toa — Tahu, Kopaka, Gali, Pohatu, Onua, Lewa, and Takanuva — stood silently around the Amaja Circle. The Turaga had used that sandpit and the stones within it many times to tell tales of the past and future.

The Turaga of Fire placed the stone representing Mata Nui in the center of the circle and began. "In the time before time, long before any Matoran set foot on the island of Mata Nui, there was a city of legends. Hear now the first tale of Metru Nui. . . ."

Kapura walked slowly along the outskirts of the district of Ta-Metru, his eyes scanning the ground. Most of the homes and factories in this part of the metru had been abandoned lately, with the residents moving closer to the heart of the district. It was Kapura's job to make sure nothing of importance had been left behind.

He paused in front of a massive, blackened building that had once housed a forge. Here, construction tools and other equipment had been cast from molten protodermis before being sent on to Po-Metru for finishing. Now, in the interest of safety, that work had been transferred away from the outskirts by order of the city's elder, Turaga Dume. Kapura spotted a staff used in the sport of kolhii on the ground and bent down to pick it up, only to discover the handle was cracked.

He walked on. This was an important task, his fellow workers had told him, and important tasks were best done slowly and carefully.

Had Kapura looked up, he would have seen the skyline of Ta-Metru, "home of the makers." Cone-shaped factories, scorched by ages of use, stood next to the homes of smiths and crafters. These were the Matoran who molded protodermis, the substance of which everything on Metru Nui was made, into thousands of shapes and forms. A molten river of raw protodermis ran through the center of the district, drawn from below the city and fed into the Great Furnace. From there, it traveled to each factory to be turned into masks, tools, and anything else that might be needed.

Dominating the skyline was the Coliseum, home to Turaga Dume and the tallest building in all of Metru Nui. For as long as anyone could remember, the sight of the Coliseum had brought a feeling of safety and security to Matoran. But now . . .

Kapura counted slowly as he walked. Six, seven, eight — at least eight of the workers at his factory had vanished lately. Where they disappeared to, and why, no one knew. But there were plenty of rumors.

The Matoran stopped. Something had moved off to the right. It didn't sound like another Matoran, or even a wild Rahi beast. It was a soft, slithering sound, as if something was dragging itself across the ground. The sound grew louder and seemed to multiply. Kapura felt the urge to run, but his feet would not move.

He forced himself to turn around and look. Four thick, blackened, twisted vines were snaking their way out of cracks in the ground, weaving in the air as if momentarily unsure of what to do. Then they wrapped themselves around the empty factory and began to climb, winding around again and again until they covered the building from top to bottom.

Kapura's eyes widened as the vines started to squeeze. Solid protodermis crumbled before their strength. The building groaned and cracked, collapsing in on itself in a matter of seconds. As if satisfied, the vines pulled away and began to move toward another structure.

It was then that Kapura found his voice. But he could speak only one word, and that in a horrified whisper:

"Morbuzakh."

In another section of the city, a second Matoran was also thinking about the dreaded Morbuzakh plant. The vines had been appearing on the outskirts of the city for some time, wrecking structures and forcing residents to flee. No one knew where they came from or how to stop them. All that was known was that everyone who challenged the Morbuzakh vanished, never to be seen again.

But this particular Matoran wasn't worried about the damage the plant was causing. Instead, all his attention was focused on a tablet decorated with a most interesting carving. The picture showed the combined power of six disks defeating a gigantic Morbuzakh root. Disks — called

Kanoka in the Matoran language — were a common sight in Metru Nui. The spheres were created in every metru and used primarily for sport, as well as for defense against the wild beasts called Rahi. Disks found to be of the right purity and power level were forged into Masks of Power. But the disks in the carving could not simply be any old Kanoka, the Matoran knew. These had to be the six Great Disks of legend.

Under the picture of each Great Disk was inscribed the section of the city where it could be found and the name of a Matoran: Nuhrii, Ahkmou, Vhisola, Tehutti, Ehrye, and Orkahm.

When he was done examining the carving, the Matoran turned to Nidhiki, the strange, four-legged being who had brought it. "What is it I'm supposed to do?"

"I would think it would be obvious," hissed Nidhiki from the shadows. "Get the six Great Disks. I don't care how. Then give them to me and I will take them somewhere . . . safe."

The Matoran frowned. "If they truly exist, these are the six most powerful Kanoka disks in

Metru Nui. They would be beyond price. What do I get out of this?"

"You will be well paid, Matoran," Nidhiki replied, smiling in a particularly nasty way. "Plus you get one more benefit, if you're successful: I won't come looking for you."

"All right, all right. I get the idea. But why is this so important? Even if these Matoran could get their hands on the Great Disks, they wouldn't dare try to stop the Morbuzakh themselves."

"It's not Matoran we're worried about," came the answer. "It's so-called heroes — Toa Metru. Six Toa Metru."

With that, Nidhiki was gone. The Matoran watched him go, thinking, *Six Toa Metru? How is that possible?*

Moments before, they had been Matoran. Six strangers, each from a different metru, brought together by a plea for help from Toa Lhikan, the hero of Metru Nui. Now, in the heart of the Great Temple in Ga-Metru, they had been transformed. Where once six Matoran had stood, there now existed six new Toa Metru.

Whenua, once an archivist in Onu-Metru and now the Toa of Earth, voiced the thoughts of them all. "Since when are Matoran just zapped into Toa?"

Nuju, former seer and now Toa of Ice, answered, "When uncertain times lie ahead."

Vakama, Ta-Metru's most skilled mask maker and the new Toa of Fire, looked down at his new form. It was hard to believe that this new power had been granted to him. He remembered the city's protector, Toa Lhikan, giving him a powerful artifact called a Toa stone and a map to a spot in the Great Temple. Then Lhikan was captured by two strange creatures, one a four-legged foe and the other huge and powerful. Heeding his last wish, Vakama had taken the Toa stone to the temple, only to run into five other Matoran with similar missions.

They placed their stones on top of the shrine dedicated to Toa. Before their eyes, the

Toa stones began to pulsate and then rose into the air. Beams of elemental energy shot from them, bathing the Matoran in light, changing them, granting them power. When it was over, the Matoran had become Toa Metru, destined guardians of Metru Nui.

But are we ready for this? Am I? Vakama asked himself. He didn't have an answer.

The other Toa had begun selecting their tools from a compartment inside the suva shrine. Vakama looked over what remained and chose a powerful Kanoka disk launcher. It was a larger version of what he had used in the past to play the sport of kolhii. The familiarity of it made him feel a little more comfortable in his new body.

Matau, Toa of Air, chuckled. "Nice choice — for playing Matoran games, mask maker."

"Hey, look at this," Onewa, the new Toa Metru of Stone, said. He reached into the tool compartment and emerged with six Kanoka disks. Each was a different color, and each bore the likeness of a Mask of Power. But what drew the attention of the new heroes was that the masks matched the ones they now wore.

"What does it mean?" asked Nokama, Toa Metru of Water.

"Perhaps that we were not chosen at random for this?" Vakama suggested. "Perhaps this is our destiny."

"What did Toa Lhikan say we could expect, Vakama? What are we meant to do now that we are Toa?" asked Whenua. Nokama and Onewa drew in closer, anxious to hear the answer as well.

"He said —" Vakama began.

Then, suddenly, his mind was somewhere else. He could see day being consumed by night, Metru Nui collapsing into ruin, then miraculously restored. Six Kanoka disks flew at him from out of the darkness, forcing him to duck and dodge. They shot past him, then hovered in the air and unleashed their power on the Morbuzakh plant. Before their energies, the plant withered and died. Their task done, the Great Disks merged together to form a single one of immense power, and . . .

Then the vision was gone. But the chill inside Vakama told him it had not just been an idle daydream. "Metru Nui was destroyed. I saw it! Six Great Kanoka Disks were headed right for me, and . . ."

"Thanks for dream-sharing," Matau said, shaking his head.

"No, we must find them. They can defeat the Morbuzakh and free the city from danger. That would prove we are worthy to be Toa Metru!" Vakama continued.

The others looked at him, some doubtful, some evidently willing to believe. They had all heard the tales of the Great Disks before. It was said they contained enormous power, but the only clue to their location was that one was hidden in each metru. If the disks were used by someone with good intent, they could change the world for the better. If their user was evil, Metru Nui and all its inhabitants might be erased forever.

"Then find them we shall," said Nokama. "I saw a carving in the temple that might help us.

Something about finding the Great Disks by seeking the unfamiliar within the familiar. But the rest seemed to be . . . riddles. What do you think, Vakama?"

But the Toa of Fire was not listening. In his mind's eye, he saw six Matoran, each with a Great Disk. He knew their names but could not see their faces. Worse, the shadows behind them were alive with danger. Vakama could see a pair of fierce red eyes hovering in the darkness and a four-legged creature stalking the Matoran. He had seen that figure before, in real life, struggling with Toa Lhikan. Vakama knew how powerful and evil this being was, and the memory made him shudder.

"Nuhrii . . . Orkahm . . . Vhisola . . . Ahkmou . . . Ehrye . . . Tehutti," Vakama muttered. "They can decipher the riddles. They can help us find the Great Disks. But beware of a dark hunter who walks on four legs."

"You have spent too much time at the forge, fire-spitter," answered Onewa. "Your head needs cooling down."

"I trust Vakama," Nokama said. "If he believes those six Matoran can help us find the disks, then we must seek them out. When we have found them, we will meet back here. Good luck to us all."

If my vision is true, thought Vakama, *we will need far, far more than luck.*

The Toa Metru said their farewells and went their separate ways. Only Nokama and Vakama remained behind, staring up at the Great Temple.

"Vakama, do you really think Metru Nui is in danger? Perhaps from something more frightening than the Morbuzakh?"

"I know there is darkness coming," Vakama replied. "Toa Lhikan said we had to stop it. He said we had to save the 'heart of the city.' I don't know how or why, but we have been chosen."

"Then may the Great Beings protect us all," said the Toa of Water.

BIONICLE®

Adventures #2

Trial by Fire

PROLOGUE

Tahu Nuva, Toa of Fire, struggled to accept all that he had heard. Many a time he had listened to Turaga Vakama, elder of the village of Ta-Koro, tell a tale of past glories. But never such a story as this.

He had asked the Turaga to share with him and his fellow heroes a tale of Metru Nui. The Toa would soon be leading the Matoran villagers to this new island. They wished to be prepared for any danger that might await them there.

The tale Vakama told was a shocking one. He revealed that he and the other village elders had, long ago, been Matoran, living in a great city on Metru Nui. Through a strange twist of fate, they were gifted with the power of Toa. Their destiny: to save their city from disaster.

"We believed Metru Nui to be a paradise," Vakama had said. "But it was a city under siege. A dark, twisted plant called the Morbuzakh threatened from every side, bringing down buildings and driving Matoran from their homes. If left unchecked, nothing would remain of the city we loved."

But how to save the city? The answer came to Vakama in a vision. The Toa Metru had to seek out six Matoran who knew the hiding places of the Great Disks. These disks, when used together, could defeat the Morbuzakh. It seemed a simple task, and one that would surely prove to all in Metru Nui that these new Toa were worthy of being called heroes.

But the six Toa faced many dangers before the Matoran could be found. Still unskilled in the use of their powers, they barely escaped traps that had been set along their way. It soon became clear that one of the Matoran was seeking to betray the others, and all of Metru Nui as well.

It was at that point that Vakama had

stopped speaking. Now the Toa had gathered again to hear more of his strange tale.

Gali Nuva, Toa of Water, approached him quietly and laid a hand on his shoulder.

"Are you ready to continue, Turaga?" she asked. "Should we wait for another time?"

Vakama shook his head. "No, Toa Gali. These secrets have been kept from you for far too long. The time has come to speak. But . . . it is not easy."

"You said that you felt sure one of the six Matoran was walking in shadow," Tahu, Toa of Fire, said. "Why didn't you turn him over to the enforcers of order in Metru Nui — what did you call them?"

"Vahki," replied Vakama. "We had no choice. Those six Matoran were the only ones who knew the location of the Great Disks, and we had to have those disks. But we knew we must take precautions against betrayal."

"Tell us more, Turaga," said Pohatu. "Continue your story, please."

"Very well, Toa of Stone," said Vakama. "Now where was I? Oh, yes. With the six Matoran having been found, we Toa Metru were ready to begin searching for the Great Disks. Time was running out — with each day, the Morbuzakh grew bolder and more of the city was brought to ruin.

"It was decided that we would split into teams to search the city for the disks, bringing the Matoran with us. Of course, not everyone was happy about this idea. . . ."

1

"Next time, I'm picking the teams," grumbled Onewa, Toa Metru of Stone. He had been trudging along behind Vakama, Toa of Fire, and two of the Matoran for the better part of an hour. He hadn't bothered to keep his unhappiness a secret.

Nuhrii said nothing. A Matoran from the Ta-Metru district, all his energies were focused on finding the disks. In his mind, he saw himself showered with praise for helping to save the city and maybe even having a Mask of Power named after him someday. Turaga Dume, elder of Metru Nui, might even want a Matoran of such courage as an advisor.

The other Matoran on the journey, Ahkmou, was a Po-Matoran carver. He turned back to look at Onewa and said, "Since when did Onewa follow the rules? Has becoming a Toa

Metru made you soft? Leave these two fire-spitters behind and let's find the Great Disk ourselves."

"Sure," grunted Onewa. "And maybe walk into another trap. Don't think I've forgotten how hard it was to catch you, Ahkmou. I trust you about as far as I could throw the Great Temple."

Vakama was tempted to tell the bickering Po-Metru natives to be quiet, but that would probably just make things worse. Maybe it had been a mistake using Kanoka disks to choose the teams. But they were easy to find, since every Matoran used disks for sport, and the three-digit codes on them offered a simple way to decide. The two lowest codes worked together, the two highest, and so on. It was just bad luck he had wound up with Onewa. They just could not seem to get along.

They had crossed the border of Ta-Metru a short while ago. Nokama, Toa Metru of Water, had found a series of clues to the locations of the Great Disks carved on the wall of the Great Temple. According to the inscription, finding the

Ta-Metru disk required "embracing the root of fire." Vakama and Nuhrii both knew what that meant, but neither wanted to speak about it out loud.

Onewa and Ahkmou looked around, uncomfortably. Their home metru was known for its wide, flat expanses where massive sculptures were carved and stored. Ta-Metru, on the other hand, was a land of fire, where molten rivers of protodermis were forged into masks, tools, and other objects. Buildings crowded in close and all of them reflected the red glow of the furnaces. The sound of crafters' tools striking in unison and the hiss of cooling masks seemed to come from every side.

"I need a rest," said Ahkmou. "My feet are tired."

"Mine too," said Nuhrii. "Why couldn't we just take the transport chutes?"

Vakama frowned. He had insisted that they travel on foot, and Onewa had agreed. Taking the chutes would make it too easy for one or both Matoran to jump out midway and disappear into the streets and alleyways. "All right. But stay to-gether and stay here."

The two Matoran sat down. Vakama walked away, expecting Onewa to keep an eye on them, but the Toa Metru of Stone followed him. "Do you know where we're going? What is this 'root of fire'?"

Vakama gestured toward the buildings that surrounded them. "Well, you know about the Great Furnace in Ta-Metru, and all the smaller furnaces and forges here. The flames that feed them come from fire pits . . . the 'roots' of the fire. They are highly dangerous places."

"Let me guess. Climbing down into one is against the law in Ta-Metru, so we're going to have Vahki squads to worry about."

"Probably."

"You had better be right about all this," Onewa said. "Or it's the last time I'm trusting you, fire-spitter."

Vakama felt anger rising in him, and this time didn't try to fight it off. "Do you have a better plan? These six disks are the only thing that can save Metru Nui. Unless we find them, the whole place is going to fall to the — Morbuzakh!"

The Toa Metru of Fire pointed over Onewa's shoulder, but his warning came too late. A twisted Morbuzakh vine snaked out of a chute and wrapped itself around Onewa, lifting the startled Toa into the air.

"My arms are pinned!" the Toa Metru of Stone shouted. "I can't get free!"

"Hang on! I'll save you!" Vakama said, thrusting a disk into his disk launcher.

"Hang on? Hang on to what??" The Morbuzakh was dragging Onewa toward the chute. Once inside, it would be too late to free him.

Vakama aimed carefully and launched his disk at the vine. When it struck, it sent bitter cold along the length of the plant, freezing it solid. With the pressure gone, Onewa was able to wriggle free. He hit the ground and looked from the vine to Vakama.

"Yeah, well," he muttered. "I could have done that myself . . . somehow." He idly swung his fist and shattered the frozen plant into a thousand icy shards.

Vakama turned and headed back toward where the Matoran waited. "You can have the next one then. Maybe if you grumble at it, it will go away."

"Hasn't worked with you," replied Onewa.

Vakama didn't answer. The spot where they had left Nuhrii and Ahkmou was empty. He felt a sinking feeling inside. If the two of them had vanished . . .

"There!" yelled Onewa. He pointed toward the two Matoran, who were fleeing in the direction of Po-Metru. The Toa of Stone whirled his proto-piton tool above his head and made a perfect throw, the cable wrapping around Ahkmou's legs. Smiling, Onewa began reeling in the Po-Matoran.

"Nice," said Vakama. "But here's an easier way." He took out a teleportation disk, checked its three-digit code to make sure it was low power, and then hurled it from his launcher. It struck Nuhrii a glancing blow and the Ta-Matoran disappeared. An instant later, he popped back into existence right in front of the two Toa.

"I guess you weren't that tired after all," said Vakama. "So let's keep moving."

"So have you ever visited these fire pits before?" Onewa asked.

"No," Vakama said softly. "Even mask makers are not allowed near them. The risk is too great."

"Scorched Matoran, right?"

"Not only that," said Vakama. "If anything happened to the flames in those pits, production in Ta-Metru would come to a halt." Seeing the lack of reaction on Onewa's face, he added, "There would be nothing for the Po-Matoran to carve."

They were working their way slowly toward the center of the city, trying to keep off the busier avenues. Onewa insisted the two Matoran stay close, while he himself kept scanning the alleys. Vakama did not need to ask why. They both could sense they were being followed.

At one point, just after they rounded a corner, Onewa gestured for them to flatten against the wall. They waited a long moment, but no one went by except the occasional Matoran. Finally, Onewa peered around the edge of the building and shook his head. "Not there."

"Who do you think it is?" asked Ahkmou.

"Guess," answered Onewa. A four-legged creature named Nidhiki had been chasing Ahkmou when Onewa found him. The same powerful being had been responsible for sabotage and traps encountered by the other Toa Metru in their search for the Matoran. Whoever he was, he did not want the Toa finding the Great Disks.

"Maybe we should get off the street," Vakama suggested. "We can take a shortcut through —"

"The protodermis reclamation furnace," Nuhrii finished. "The rear exit would bring us out near the fire pits."

"Lead the way," said Onewa. "All these fires, flames, and furnaces look alike to me."

* * *

The protodermis reclamation furnace was relatively small as Ta-Metru furnaces went, but its fires were just as hot and had plenty to burn. Damaged masks, tools and other items were sent here from the reclamation yard to be melted down. The resulting liquid protodermis was then fed through special channels back to the forges, where it could be used again. What went into the furnace was little more than garbage, but what came out might become something wonderful in the hands of a skilled crafter.

Its function made it ideal for use as a shortcut to the fire pits. For one thing, the place ran itself. Few, if any, Matoran actually worked there, so the building would most likely be empty. The Nuurakh, the Ta-Metru Vahki squads, did not bother patrolling in the area. After all, who would want to steal trash?

Vakama led the way as they slipped into the side entrance. The only light inside came from the fire in the furnace. The building consisted of a wide catwalk that ran along all four sides and looked down upon a long chute. The chute ran through the center of the building, carrying items directly from the yards to the flames. The air inside was heavy with smoke and the smell of melting protodermis.

Onewa walked to the edge of the catwalk and peered down. He had never seen anything like this. In his home district of Po-Metru, goods arrived already shaped, and carvers added the finishing touches. Watching masks and tools move slowly through a chute toward destruction was incredible, and even a little frightening.

Vakama joined him. "Sometimes I am not sure I like this place."

"Why not?"

"It keeps us from learning from our mistakes. We just melt them down and make them go away."

"Toa! Watch out!"

Neither Vakama nor Onewa had time to react to Nuhrii's shout. Twin blasts of energy struck them, sending them tumbling over the catwalk and through the energized walls of the chute. They hit hard and lay there, stunned, as the chute moved them closer and closer to the white-hot flames.

Nidhiki stepped out of the shadows. The two Matoran had run away, but there would be time to find them later. For now, he wanted to enjoy his victory over the two Toa Metru. He looked down at the unmoving forms of Vakama and Onewa, his dark laughter mingling with the crackling of the flames.

BIONICLE®

Adventures #3

The Darkness
Below

INTRODUCTION

Jaller paused from his labors for a moment and took a deep breath. He could not remember ever working harder than he had in the past few days. Ever since it had been announced that the Matoran were going to move from the island of Mata Nui to the island city of Metru Nui, villagers had been toiling day and night to build enough boats for the great journey.

For Jaller and his friends, the nonstop work was welcome. Their home, Ta-Koro, had been destroyed in the battle to save the island from darkness, and they were living in other villages until the time came to leave Mata Nui forever. Talk around the fires at night was about Metru Nui, what wonders they might find there, and how soon they would be able to leave for this new and mysterious place.

"We'll never get to Metru Nui if the great Jaller keeps taking rest breaks."

Jaller turned to see his friend Hahli smiling at him. The Ga-Matoran had recently been named the new Chronicler, and ever since she had been traveling from place to place gathering tales about Metru Nui. She hoped to be able to share the stories with the other Matoran during the long journey to come.

"At least when I'm working, I'm *working*," replied Jaller good-naturedly. "You can't build a boat with a story, you know."

"Maybe not, but it sure makes the sailing go faster. I'm heading to see Turaga Vakama. He's about to continue his tale of Metru Nui to the Toa. I am supposed to record it for the Wall of History we will build on the new island. Come with me?"

Jaller thought about it. He probably should keep working, but he was already far ahead of all the others. It wouldn't do any harm to take a little time off.

"Okay. Let's go," he said.

The two of them set out for the Amaja Circle sandpit, the place where Turaga Vakama traditionally told his tales. After a short while, Jaller asked, "So is it true?"

"Is what true?"

"All the stories I have been hearing. How the Turaga were once Toa on Metru Nui; how they searched for six missing Matoran, but learned that one of the Matoran planned to betray the city; and how they gathered six Great Disks and used them to defeat a menace called the Morbuzakh."

Hahli nodded. "Yes, it's all true. Amazing, isn't it? One moment, they were Matoran just like us, living and working in a great city. The next moment, they were Toa Metru with powers and Toa tools and everything!"

Up ahead, they could see the seven Toa gathered around Turaga Vakama. The Turaga had already begun to speak. "It had been a difficult and dangerous mission, but we six Toa Metru had triumphed. Metru Nui had been saved from the Morbuzakh, and we were certain that we would be hailed as heroes. But we were about to face another test, one that would threaten to shatter our newfound unity."

The Turaga of Fire turned his gaze to the night sky, but all present knew that his eyes were truly viewing images from the past. "Toa would challenge Toa in the darkness below the city, in a struggle that still lives in my nightmares."

The six Toa Metru walked through the streets of Ta-Metru, on their way to the Coliseum. For the first time since they had transformed from Matoran, they felt no need to travel by way of back alleys or to stay in the shadows. Even the presence of Vahki, Metru Nui's order enforcement squads, did not worry them. After all, they had just defeated the Morbuzakh plant that menaced the city. They were heroes!

Better still, they had found the legendary Great Disks, which had been hidden in separate parts of the city. They had no doubt that these artifacts would be enough to convince the city's elder, Turaga Dume, and all the Matoran that here were new Toa capable of defeating any threat.

"They will cheer-hail us in the Coliseum," said Matau, Toa of Air, with a grin. "Po-Metru carvers will make statues of us. Perhaps they will even rename the districts for us! 'Ma-Metru' — I like the ring-sound of that!"

The other Toa laughed. Matau was exaggerating, of course, but certainly Turaga Dume would honor them in some way. Matoran all over the city would demand it.

"With the Morbuzakh gone, maybe we won't have any dangers to face," offered Whenua, Toa of Earth. "Except for the occasional Rahi beast on the loose, Metru Nui is usually pretty peaceful."

"Just rest on our reputations, huh, Whenua?" said Onewa, Toa of Stone. "Not me. Now that I'm a Toa Metru, I'm going to take advantage of it. The best tools, the best materials, mine for the asking — I'll build statues like you have never seen before!"

"I will do many Toa-hero deeds," said Matau. "That way there will always be tales to tell about me. What about you, Nokama?"

"Well, I'm not sure," replied the Toa of Water. "There are so many places to see and explore. What is it like under the sea? What lies beyond the sky? Where do all those strange creatures you see in the Onu-Metru Archives come from? Now I have the power to go wherever I please and learn those answers."

Nuju, Toa of Ice, shrugged. "I don't feel any need to explore. I have more than enough to keep me busy in Ko-Metru. Now that I am a Toa, perhaps others will not be so quick to interrupt me when I am working."

Only Vakama, Toa of Fire, had yet to speak. Of all the Toa Metru, he was the least comfortable with his new powers and the responsibilities that came with them. Still, when duty demanded it, he had risen to the occasion and led the Toa to victory. Nokama noticed his silence and asked, "What about you, Vakama? Surely you have some dream you want to realize now that you are a Toa?"

"Not really," he answered. "I mean, I am glad we became Toa and were able to save the city. But . . . I would be just as happy to still be working at my forge in Ta-Metru. It was much simpler. I guess once a mask-maker, always a mask-maker."

Onewa chuckled. "The fire-spitter wants to go back to being a Matoran. I don't think the transformation works in the opposite direction."

"Yes, we are stuck being Toa-heroes," said Matau. "And so many worry-problems we have — how many bows to take? How many mask-sculptures in each metru? How big of a shelter-house for each of us?"

"If you aren't happy being a Toa, Vakama, maybe we should choose a new leader," said Onewa. "I am sure I could do the job."

"Or I!" said Matau. "Matau of Ma-Metru, leader of the Toa-heroes! Oh, I like that!"

"I never said I didn't want to be a Toa," Vakama said. "And I *never* said I wanted to be the leader. I did the job because I knew Ta-Metru better than any of you. If someone else wants to be leader, go ahead."

Nokama looked at Vakama. She could tell that he was hurt by the things Onewa and Matau were saying, but he wasn't going to admit to it. As they walked, the other Toa Metru debated who was best qualified to lead the team. Onewa said it should be a creative thinker like him. Matau countered that a high-flyer was best qualified to plan strategy. Whenua said he would take the job if asked, then seemed disappointed when no one asked him.

As for Nuju, the Toa of Ice summed up his feelings in a few words. "I don't care who leads us, as long as he doesn't expect me to follow."

Nokama was about to put all four of them in their place when she saw a Matoran approaching at a run. He was from Onu-Metru, and the anxious look on his face said there was serious trouble somewhere.

Whenua stepped forward to greet him. The Matoran's name was Nuparu, and he was not someone Whenua knew well. When other workers in the Archives were busy among the exhibits, Nuparu was off on his own tinkering. He was always trying to figure out how Gukko birds flew, how the great Muaka cat could stretch its neck to lunge at prey, and other questions that might seem trivial to others. Still, Nuparu leaving the Archives and hurrying into Ta-Metru was enough to catch the Toa of Earth's attention.

"Toa! The Archives are in danger!" the Matoran shouted.

"It's all right, Nuparu," said Whenua. "The Morbuzakh has been defeated. Everyone is safe."

The Matoran shook his head frantically. "No, no, it's not the Morbuzakh. It's the sea! It's going to flood the Archives and destroy all of the exhibits!"

Whenua wasn't sure how to react to the Matoran's words. The Onu-Metru digging machines, and the workers who operated them, took special care to make sure the outer walls of the Archives were reinforced. The deeper they dug to create new sublevels, the greater the pressure from the liquid protodermis outside. But the sea had never posed a serious threat to the existence of the exhibits in all of Metru Nui's recorded history.

The Toa of Earth waved the other Toa Metru away. This was an Onu-Metru problem, and would be solved by the guardian of that district, he decided. "Now tell me what you saw," he said to Nuparu.

"I was down . . . um . . . below the sublevels, and —"

"Wait a moment, what were you doing so far down? You know how risky it is to go there!" As soon as he said it, Whenua regretted the sharpness of his tone. But it had not been so long ago that he had been down in that dark and fearsome section, and he had barely escaped intact. No Onu-Matoran, archivist or not, had any business wandering among "exhibits" deemed too dangerous for display.

"Well, I . . . I . . . I heard there was a Rahkshi down there, a yellow one, and it had been defeated, and I wanted to . . . well . . ."

"You were hoping to scavenge some parts for your latest invention," Whenua finished for him, frowning. "You know what would happen if the other archivists caught you doing that? Or worse, a Vahki?"

"I know," Nuparu said, looking down at his

feet. "But I didn't find anything anyway. Then I saw a hatch in the floor and I went down through it. There was a whole maze of tunnels there I never knew existed! So I used my lightstone to explore. I didn't see very much, no exhibits or anything, but when I rounded a corner, I was suddenly walking in protodermis! The sea was leaking in!"

Nuparu's voice was loud enough that the other Toa Metru could not help but hear. Nokama, in particular, was intrigued by the mention of the sea. She drew closer as the Matoran continued to talk.

"So at first I didn't know what to think. I was going to turn back, but then I figured as long as I was down there, I'd better find out how serious the situation was. I found one whole wall had a huge crack and the sea was pouring right through it!"

"How bad?"

"The crack is spreading. If it's not repaired soon, the whole sea wall will breach," said Nuparu. "The sublevels will flood, then the lower levels, and pretty soon the whole Archives will be washed away."

"But there is a repair crew headed down now, right?"

Nuparu shook his head. "No one wants to go down there. They've all heard too many stories. That's why, when I heard there was a new Toa of Earth, I came looking for you. Someone has to do something!"

"Someone will," replied Whenua. "Now tell me the story again. I want to hear every detail of what you saw, and where you saw it."

Nokama had rejoined the others by the time Whenua was finished talking with the Matoran. The Toa of Earth looked grim as he walked over to the group.

"I have to go," he said. "Someone will have to apologize to Turaga Dume for me, but this is an emergency. I'll meet you all at the Coliseum later on."

"What could be more serious-matter than telling the world what we can do?" asked Matau.

"Actually doing it," Nokama answered. "But you don't have to take on this task alone. I will come with you. The Archives are important to everyone in Metru Nui. I know anyone from Ga-Metru would do the same."

"I'll come too," said Vakama. "My flame power is weak after the struggle with the Morbuzakh, but maybe I can help somehow." He turned to Onewa. "Can you three explain to Turaga Dume why we cannot present ourselves to him just yet?"

"Oh, sure," Onewa snorted. "'The other three of us would be here, Turaga, but they're out being heroes while we stand around.' I say we *all* go, we *all* do the job, and then we *all* head to the Coliseum. What do you think? Matau? Nuju?"

"The sooner we take care of all this, the sooner I can get back to Ko-Metru," said Nuju. "I say we help Whenua."

"Hmmmmmm," Matau said. "I was in a hurry to tell the Matoran we are Toa-heroes now. But I suppose repair-saving the Archives along with the whole city will be good for twice the celebration. On to Onu-Metru!"

Their course of action agreed upon, the six changed direction and began journeying toward the metru of the archivists. Whenua led the way, still talking with Nuparu, while Nokama and Vakama brought up the rear. After a short while, the Toa of Water said, "You know, we cannot take a vote every time we have to decide something."

"What's that?"

"Just now. The protodermis could have risen another level in the time it took for each Toa to decide if he was coming along or not. We don't have the luxury of debating every point. We need a leader."

"I'm sure you'll do a fine job," he said.

"No, that's not what I —" Nokama began, but the Toa of Fire had already walked away.

BIONICLE®

Adventures #4

Legends of
Metru Nui

INTRODUCTION

Turaga Vakama stood on a natural stone balcony that looked out over a vast silver sea. Directly in front of him was an Amaja circle, the sand pit used by Turaga for ages to tell stories of the past. Now, surrounded by his fellow Turaga, the Matoran villagers, the six Toa Nuva and Takanuva, Toa of Light, he was about to tell the most important tale of all.

"Gathered friends," he began. "Listen again to our legend of the Bionicle. In the time before time, in the glorious city of Metru Nui, we believed new heroes could not be made.

"But we were wrong."

Vakama moved the stone that represented the Great Spirit, Mata Nui, to the center of the circle. Now the lightstones began to flicker and darkness shrouded the sand pit.

"An unrelenting shadow sought to enforce endless sleep," Vakama continued, "until memories of times past were lost. Then he could create a time of dark order, and awaken the world as its conqueror."

Vakama raised his eyes to the heavens, remembering a time long ago. "Hope, it seemed, was lost."

Toa Lhikan, guardian of the city of Metru Nui, stood in the semi-darkness of the Great Temple. He had come here many times in the past to remember what had gone before and reflect on the future. This had always been a place that had soothed his spirit. But not today.

The errand that had brought him to one of the most revered sites in Metru Nui was one that filled him with sadness and doubt. Many a night he had wondered if there might be some other way, but no other answer presented itself. Finally, he admitted that he had no choice. It had to be done, and done now, before it was too late.

Grimly, Lhikan pried open the suva. Then he reached in and took the sixth and last Toa stone off its pedestal.

As he had done five times before, Toa Lhikan

placed the stone on a thin sheet of metallic pro-todermis in his open palm. Then he clenched his fist, wrapping the sheet tightly around the stone.

Behind his yellow Great Mask of Shielding, Lhikan's eyes narrowed. He knew that he was doing far more than taking valuable objects of power. He was taking a step that would change his life, the lives of six others, and the very future of Metru Nui.

He held his other hand over his closed fist and concentrated. Six streams of energy came from his hand, then merged into a single white lance of power. It flowed over the wrapped Toa stone, then abruptly came to a stop. When Lhikan opened his fist, he saw that the metallic sheet was now sealed around the stone. Imprinted upon it was the symbol of the three virtues of the Matoran: Unity, Duty, and Destiny.

Lhikan heard a soft sound behind him and turned quickly. Approaching from out of the darkness were two figures, one a four-legged insectoid being, the other a hulking brute. Lhikan knew all too well who they were and why they were here. He was already moving as the insectoid began hurling energy blasts.

Fleeing was against Lhikan's nature, but he had been a Toa long enough to know it did not pay to challenge impossible odds. He ran, dodging as the two Dark Hunters attempted to snare him in energy webs. As they closed in, the Toa of Fire leaped through a window and plunged into space.

The insectoid Dark Hunter rushed to the window to watch his enemy fall. Instead, he saw Lhikan combine his tools to form a glider board. Seconds later, the Toa was lost from view.

Nokama stood near the Great Temple, surrounded by her students. As a teacher, she knew it was important to get her class out of the classroom now and then, and let them see some of Metru Nui's history for themselves. Using her trident, she pointed out some of the ancient carvings on the walls of the temple.

Behind her, she could hear her students gasp. She turned to see Toa Lhikan. He approached her, handed her a small package, and then was gone. Nokama shook her head, wondering what it could all mean.

In a Po-Metru assemblers' village, Onewa was hard at work finishing a piece of carving. He had been laboring in the heat all day, but hardly noticed the time or the effort. It was all worth it when the work was done and another fine display of craftsmanship was ready to ship out. He knew that each Po-Matoran crafter in the huts around him felt the same, except perhaps Ahkmou. That one seemed more worried about how many honors he would receive than how much work he finished.

Something landed with a sharp thud on the ground at Onewa's feet. It was a small package wrapped in what looked like foil. Onewa looked up just in time to see the departing form of Toa Lhikan.

*   *   *

Whenua was content. A new shipment of Bohrok had arrived at the Archives. As soon as he was done cataloging the creatures, they would be ready to go on exhibit for all Matoran to see.

He worked quickly, sorting through the items in a pile of artifacts. Some were slated for immediate exhibit, others would be sent down to the sublevels, and still more were too damaged to be of any use. These would be sent to Ta-Metru to be melted down.

Whenua was so absorbed by his work that he never heard Toa Lhikan's approach. The Toa paused only long enough to hand the Matoran a small object, then he was gone. Whenua looked in wonder at the package, whose covering glittered even in the dim light of the Archives.

Matau took a deep breath. This was his favorite part of the job — testing new vehicles before they hit the streets of Le-Metru. He was, naturally, the best qualified to run them around the test track, being the most highly skilled rider in the entire metru . . . at least, in his opinion.

Today's test vehicle was a one-Matoran moto-sled invented by an Onu-Matoran named Nuparu. He claimed it would someday replace the Ussal crabs that carried cargo to and fro in Metru Nui. Matau was less worried about that than about how fast it could go.

When the signal was given, Matau worked the controls and the machine began to move. Soon it was racing around the test track. Matau smiled, certain that he could coax a little more speed out of Nuparu's machine. He reached out, grabbed one of the controls — and it broke off in his hand.

Matau's eyes went wide. *Oh, this is not happy-cheer at all*, he thought.

All around him, pieces of the vehicle were flying off as the vehicle spun madly. Finally, only the control seat remained, with Matau hanging on to keep from being tossed the length of the track. Sparks flew as the lone intact section skidded to a halt, and Matau jumped off at the last possible moment.

The Matoran managed not to break anything on his landing. As he rose to his feet, he saw he was not alone. Toa Lhikan was standing beside him, offering him a gift. Then the Toa was gone.

Matau looked at the small, heavy item in his hand. *Truly an ever-strange day*, he said to himself.

Nuju peered through his telescope. From his vantage point high atop a Ko-Metru tower, he could see the sky, the stars, Toa Lhikan gliding toward him —

Toa Lhikan?

The lone protector of Metru Nui landed softly beside the Matoran. Without a word, he handed Nuju a wrapped Toa stone. Then, secure that the coast was clear, Lhikan leaped from the roof and surfed away on the wind.

Nuju watched him go, wondering what this event might mean for his future.

Vakama carefully moved a Kanoka disk from his worktable into the fires of the forge. He watched intently as the flames softened the disk. When he felt the time was right, he removed it from the heat and began to shape it with his firestaff. He smoothed the rough edges of the disk, added eyeholes, and then paused to look at the Mask of Power he had created.

Far below him, a pool of molten protodermis bubbled and hissed. This was the raw material that was fed into the forge to be shaped into disks, and later into masks, if the grade of disk was high enough. All around was a series of interlocking catwalks, with a great crane suspended above the center of the molten vat.

Vakama held the mask up to the light and searched for flaws in the workmanship. Finding none, he placed it on his face. Given that it was a Great Mask, he knew he would not be able to access its powers, but he could at least get a sense of whether it was active. But when he donned it, it merely glowed dimly before flickering out.

Disgusted, Vakama took it off and threw it on top of a huge pile of similar masks. At the rate he was going, his stack of failures would soon be taller than he was. Shaking his head, he turned to see Toa Lhikan standing before him.

"Making Great Masks, Vakama?" asked the Toa.

Vakama took a step backward and stumbled. "Toa Lhikan! Um, not yet . . . but with the right disk . . ."

"The city needs your help," said Lhikan, reaching behind him to retrieve something. A moment later Vakama saw it was a small package wrapped in a shiny material.

"My help?" the Matoran said, taking another step backward. He bumped into the discard pile, causing the rejected masks to clatter to the floor.

"Matoran are vanishing," Lhikan continued urgently. "Deceit lurks in the shadows of Metru Nui."

"Toa — so dramatic."

Both Lhikan and Vakama turned at the voice. A large, four-legged, insectoid creature stood inside the foundry. "Always playing the hero," the creature hissed.

"Some of us take our duty seriously, Nidhiki," growled Lhikan. Then he turned to Vakama, gestured to the package, and whispered, "Keep it safe. Get to the Great Temple."

Nidhiki raised his claws. "This time your farewell will be forever, brother."

"You lost the right to call me brother long ago," said Lhikan.

Nidhiki spat blasts of dark energy. Lhikan narrowly evaded them, but one surge of energy struck the support for the catwalk, shearing through it. Lhikan was considering his next move when there came a crash from above. He looked up to see a mammoth form falling toward him.

"Time's up, Toa!" bellowed the plummeting figure.

Nidhiki smiled as his bestial partner, Krekka, crashed onto the catwalk beside Lhikan. Immediately, Toa and Dark Hunter began to grapple. Krekka's size and strength gave him the edge, but in Lhikan he faced the veteran of a thousand conflicts. The Toa waited for the right moment, then sidestepped and used Krekka's force against him. With one smooth motion, Lhikan tossed Krekka over the side of the catwalk.

The Dark Hunter might not have been the brightest being in Metru Nui, but even he knew what would happen if he landed in the vat of molten protodermis. His hand shot out and grabbed onto the edge of the catwalk, and he began to pull himself back up.

Lhikan glanced toward Vakama. The Matoran had been watching the struggle, so frozen with shock that he had not noticed the damage done by Nidhiki's earlier blast. But Lhikan could see that the catwalk on which Vakama stood was about to collapse.

"Vakama! Move!" he shouted.

It was already too late. Metal groaned and snapped and the catwalk broke free of its supports, sending Vakama sliding toward molten doom. Ignoring the threat of Nidhiki, Lhikan jumped to the broken platform and grabbed hold of the Matoran.

Nidhiki's eyes narrowed. "Compassion was always your weakness, brother," he said.

Lhikan struggled to haul Vakama back up to relative safety. Then he suddenly felt himself seized and lifted into the air. The Toa turned to see that Krekka had taken control of the crane, and it was that which now dangled Lhikan and Vakama over the bubbling vat. "It's swim time!" snarled Krekka.

The Dark Hunter shifted the controls and began to lower the crane toward the vat. Lhikan summoned all his strength, and hoisted Vakama high so the Matoran could grab onto the clawlike end of the crane. "Don't let go," the Toa ordered.

"Wasn't planning to," Vakama replied.

That had been the easy part. Now Toa Lhikan started to swing his body back and forth like a pendulum, trying to build up enough force to execute his only possible plan. He didn't think about what would happen if he failed, or about the molten substance waiting below — his entire focus was on the timing and speed of his swing.

At the crucial moment, Lhikan let go of the crane and went sailing through the air. He landed on top of the machine's cab, much to the surprise of Krekka. Before the Dark Hunter could react, Lhikan had shouldered him aside and stopped the crane's descent.

The Toa had no chance to celebrate his triumph. An energy web launched by Nidhiki wrapped around Lhikan, trapping him. As he struggled in vain to escape, his eyes locked on the Matoran.

"Vakama, the Great Spirit depends on you!" he cried. "Save the heart of Metru Nui!"

Krekka released an arc of dark energy that bound the Toa's hands, but Vakama could no longer see. His mind had been overtaken by a vision of the future. . . .

Time slowing, slowing, almost coming to a stop. A face coming closer, but obscured by waves of elemental energy. Now it became clearer . . . it was

Lhikan ... but twisted and distorted ... and behind him, a pair of red eyes that radiated pure evil ...

The horrifying sight snapped Vakama out of his trance, but left him weak and trembling. He glanced around dazedly, and was just in time to see Lhikan being dragged off by Krekka and Nidhiki. "Time is short!" yelled Lhikan. "Stop the darkness!"

"No!" Vakama shouted. For, in truth, there was nothing else he could do.